DISCARD

Fred's Beds

Barbara Samuels

Farrar Straus Giroux
New York

In memory of my friend Barbara Goldner,
who loved her beagle, Sammy

Farrar Straus Giroux Books for Young Readers
175 Fifth Avenue, New York 10010

Copyright © 2014 by Barbara Samuels
All rights reserved
Color separations by Bright Arts (H.K.) Ltd.
Printed in China by Toppan Leefung Printing Ltd.,
Dongguan City, Guangdong Province
Designed by Andrew Arnold
First edition, 2014
1 3 5 7 9 10 8 6 4 2

mackids.com

Library of Congress Cataloging-in-Publication Data
Samuels, Barbara.
    Fred's beds / Barbara Samuels. — 1st ed.
        p.   cm.
    Summary: Zelda's beagle, Fred, has many napping places, which he makes
great use of before, during, and after her birthday party.
    ISBN 978-0-374-31813-0
    [1. Beds—Fiction.   2. Beagle (Dog breed)—Fiction.   3. Dogs—
Fiction.   4. Birthdays—Fiction.   5. Parties—Fiction.]   I. Title.

PZ7.S1925Fre 2013
[E]—dc22
                                                                    2011012933

Farrar Straus Giroux Books for Young Readers may be purchased for business or promotional use.
For information on bulk purchases please contact Macmillan Corporate and Premium Sales Department
at (800) 221-7945 x5442 or by email at specialmarkets@macmillan.com.

Zelda's dog, Fred,
can sleep almost anywhere.

The Doormat Bed

The doormat is the perfect spot to keep a lookout for Zelda and the groceries.

Fred waddles inside.

"Could there be something here for me?" Fred wonders.

He investigates.

"Hmm, what's this?" He had
been hoping for something to eat.

But there is nothing for Fred, nothing at all.
At times like these, Fred needs a nap.

Some dogs have fancy beds. NOT Fred.
He curls up inside one of the shopping bags
and sighs.

Soon he is dreaming about
eating lamb chops with Zelda.

The Shopping-Bag Bed

When Fred wakes up, something messy and fun is
going on in the kitchen. Is it snowing?

Fred plops down by the counter.
If he stays very still, a treat may
fall his way.

The Pile-of-Old-Newspapers Bed

Zelda leaves the kitchen and Fred follows. Soon the smell of roses fills the air, along with the big bubbles Fred likes to pop with his nose.

"Can there be anything better than life with Zelda?"
thinks Fred, as he drifts off to sleep.

The Slightly-Soggy-Bath-Towel Bed

It isn't long before the doorbell is ringing.
So many little people!

So many sticky little hands!

Uh-oh!

So many things to eat! Fred wonders if the roses
on the cake taste better than the ones in the garden.

There's a rose on Fred's nose.

He's in big trouble.

He sees the perfect place to hide.

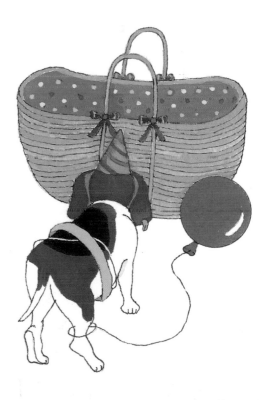

But . . .

TIME-OUT!

Zelda says Fred has been a BAD DOG. He has put his nose in the cake! He has made a baby cry!

Now he must go to the backyard and think about it!

Fred does NOT want to think
about it!

He would rather look for the beef
jerky he buried last week.

But digging is hard work.

Exhausted, he collapses into a patch of
periwinkles and petunias.

The Flower Bed

Back inside, the guests are getting restless.

They burst into the backyard.

They holler and screech.

They wake up Fred.

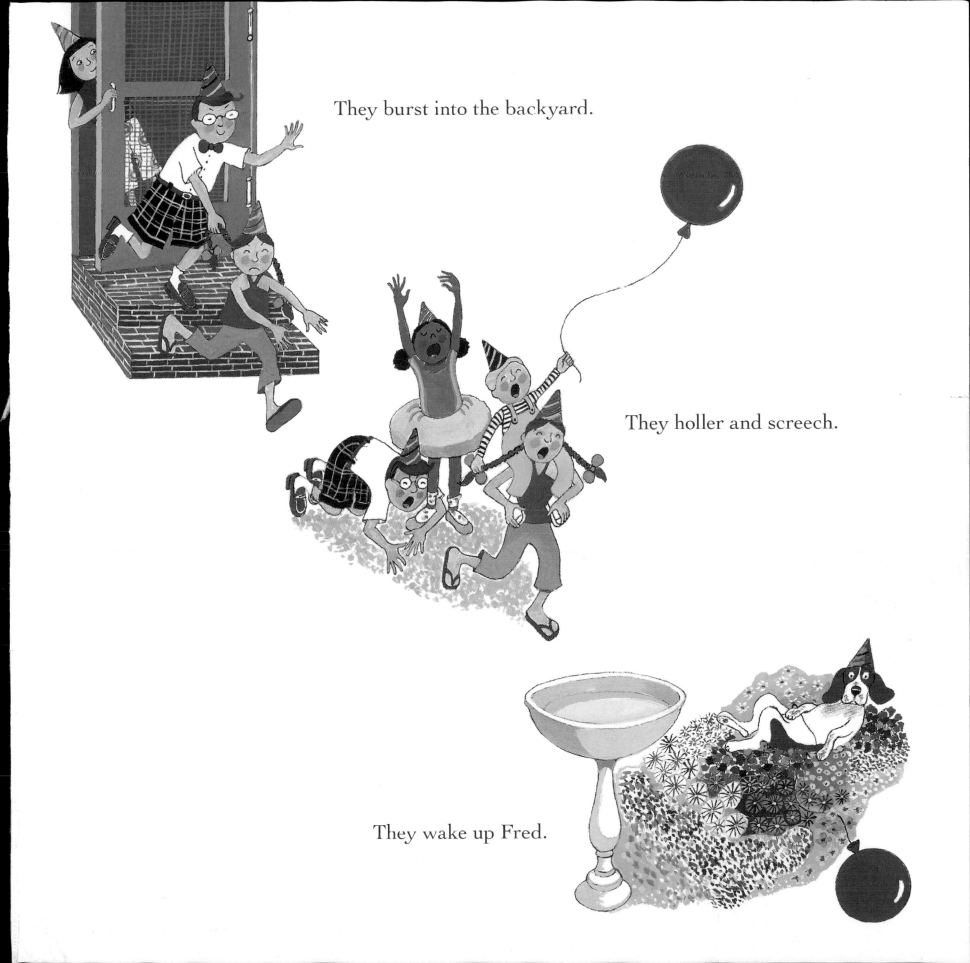

"That beagle is toast!" shouts
the boy with the bow tie.

"KEEP YOUR
HANDS OFF MY
DOG!" cries Zelda.

The guests are coming closer. Fred can smell the
pizza on their breath.

Fred makes a narrow
escape . . .

and bolts down to the
basement . . .

where he can hear his heart thumping in the dark.

The Used-to-Be-Fresh-Laundry Bed

Finally, it's quiet.
The guests are gone.

Zelda cleans Fred up.

And shows him the presents. Surprise!
One of them is for Fred.

The Brand-New Bed

Later, Zelda tucks Fred into his cozy new bed and turns out the light.

Zelda's dog, Fred, can sleep
ALMOST anywhere.

The Best Bed